BERNARD WABER

GINA

HOUGHTON MIFFLIN COMPANY BOSTON

for Mason, Anna and Rachel

Walter Lorraine (wr) Books

For information about this and other Houghton Mifflin trade
and reference books and multimedia products, visit the Bookstore
at Houghton Mifflin on the World Wide Web at
http://www.hmco.com/trade/.

Library of Congress Cataloging-in-Publication Data

Waber, Bernard.
   Gina / written and illustrated by Bernard Waber.
       p.   cm.
   Summary: When Gina moves to a new apartment building, she
discovers that there are plenty of boys but no girls her own age to
play with.
   RNF   ISBN 0-395-74279-X   PAP ISBN 0-395-87481-5
   [1. Friendship — Fiction.   2. Moving, Household — Fiction.
3. Stories in rhyme.]   I. Title.
PZ8.3.W1314Gi 1995   95-982
[E] — dc20   CIP
                          AC

Printed in the United States of America
WOZ   10   9   8   7   6   5   4   3   2

When Gina moved to an apartment in Queens . . .

. . .the girls in her building were mostly teens.
Others were still in the sandbox stage.
Oddly, there were no girls Gina's age.

Yet, and more oddly still,
there were boys, boys, boys galore,
boys, boys, boys—Gina's age,
on every floor.

Upstairs and downstairs, front and back,

lived Brian, Ryan, Tyler, and Zach.

Nicky, Ricky, Rocky, and Wally,

Alvin, Calvin, Sam, and Pasquale.

Paul, Gus, Vince, and good gracious,

Theo and his cousins, Stan and Ignatius.

Michael R., Michael V., Michael M., and Michael G.

Kyle, Lyle, Vic, and Stu. Tom, John, and Zbigniew.

Yusuf, Yakov, Laird, and Sonny. If it weren't so weird, it could have been funny.

Joshua, Rod, Mason, and Gary.

Ben, Glen, Jason, and Larry.

Ray, R.J., Jess, and Earl.
Oh, what a mess, not even one girl!

Next door to Gina, in apartment 2F,
lived Simon, Zeke, Elijah, and Jeff.
Terry, Perry, Leo (or Lee),
lived to the right in apartment 2D.

And there were the Lopezes just down the hall,
with their sons Miguel, Ricardo, and baby Raul.
Also the Garfunkels with their Kenny and Lenny.
How could there possibly be so many?

Boys, boys, boys—
clicky, clubby, birds of a feather,
wanting only to hang out together.

And there was Gina, so completely surrounded,
she could hardly remember how a girl's name sounded.
Shopping with her parents often bored her.
She tried making friends, but the boys just ignored her.

Day after day, Gina played all alone.
No friends rang her bell, or called on the phone.

She passed time drawing spaceships,
and creatures—all sorts.
She clipped pictures of athletes,
and liked books about sports.

Her only companion was Paloma the cat.
Gina loved Paloma, but wanted more than that.

And even Paloma withdrew to a shelf,
choosing at times to be unto herself.

Back in Gina's old neighborhood,
playing with kids was no big deal—
just whoever was around,
Jake, Anna, Rachel, Howie, or Abigail.

One day—
was it Nate or was it Joe?
Well, anyway, Gina told one of them
she could throw.
"Yeah, yeah," said Nate or Joe,
"here's the ball, do you really think so?"

Gina said she'd sure like trying,
and then threw a ball, that really went flying.

"Wow!" yelled the boys.
"Did you see that!
Let's give Gina
a shot at bat."

Gina clutched the bat and, with a determined face,
slammed the ball right over third base.

"Gina! Gina!" the boys
all started to scream.
"Come on over
and play on our team."

Gina made many friends that day.
Her whole life changed in every way.
Moving to the apartment was no longer a bummer.
Gina began having fun, fun, fun that summer.

Gina was always running, jumping, climbing, and hopping.
She played all day, never thinking of stopping.

She could spin on her bike
and do other good tricks,
win playing marbles
or Pickup Sticks.

Gina was always the one with ideas:
"Let's climb trees.
Let's bang pots."

And with gentler souls:
"Let's look for caterpillars.
Let's collect rocks."

Gina even stood up to mean Gootch Gibbs,
who went around picking on little kids.
With hands on her hips, she stared Gootch in the eyes,
and told him to pick on someone his size.

"Horray for Gina!" the boys began shouting
as Gootch slunk off puffing and pouting.

Gina soon had three best friends,
Alexander, Max, and Cyrus,
who called and sent get-well cards
when Gina was home with a virus.

At Gina's birthday party
her parents gave her a game,
a book, a coloring kit,
and—wow! what she wanted most—
a catcher's mitt.

Although her life was full,
Gina clung to a dream
of someday seeing other girls
play on her team.

One day, when the weather grew cool,
Gina's mother said,
"Soon, Gina,
you will be back in school."

And then Gina's mother sat down at her machine,
and sewed a blouse for Gina of emerald green.

On the first day of school, at a quarter to eight,
Gina's mother helped her dress so she wouldn't be late.
She brushed Gina's hair and made two fat braids,
tying the ends to make sure the braids stayed.

Gina was balky and squirmy, and stuck out her jaw,
but she glanced in the mirror and liked who she saw.

When Gina got on the school bus,
the boys asked, "Who's the new kid in green?
And by the way, has anyone seen
Gina?"

Gina whipped out her baseball cap
and plopped it jauntily on her head,
"Hey, guys, it's me,
Gina," she said.

"Gina!" the boys called out,
"you really look cool."

And the bus took off,
for the first day of school.